THE ADVENTURES OF HARRY STEVENSON

Guinea Pig SUPERSTAR!

KT-362-390

ALI PYE

SIMON & SCHUSTER

**For Rupert Balch and
his lovely mum and dad.**

First published in Great Britain in 2020
by Simon & Schuster UK Ltd,
A CBS COMPANY.

1 3 5 7 9 10 8 6 4 2

Simon & Schuster UK Ltd
1st Floor, 222 Gray's Inn Road, London WC1X 8HB

www.simonandschuster.co.uk
www.simonandschuster.com.au
www.simonandschuster.co.in

Simon & Schuster Australia, Sydney
Simon & Schuster India, New Delhi

A CIP catalogue record for this book is available from the British Library.

PB ISBN 978-1-4711-7025-6
EBook ISBN 978-1-4711-7026-3

Printed in China

THE ADVENTURES OF HARRY STEVENSON

Guinea Pig SUPERSTAR!

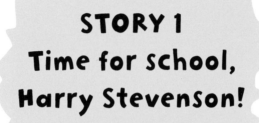

STORY 1
Time for school,
Harry Stevenson!

CHAPTER 1

Good morning,
Harry Stevenson

It was the kind of bright, sunny morning when everything looks sparkly and clean. Harry Stevenson, a plump ginger guinea pig, was no exception. Harry was having a wash. First he sat up on his hind legs and licked his front paws, then he used them to smooth down his floppy ears, brush over his ginger coat and comb out his long, silky whiskers. Cleaning his face was easy enough, but reaching round to nibble at the fur on his back was getting increasingly tricky. *I wonder why?* puzzled Harry, when he'd finished. *Perhaps I'm still growing, like Billy is*, he thought, while busily tucking into his third juicy carrot of the day.

Harry Stevenson wanted to look his best because it was a Very Special Day – one he'd been looking forward to all week. Harry still couldn't believe his luck. For as long as he could remember, he'd watched sadly from his cage on weekdays as his best friend, Billy Smith, packed his bag and headed off to a place called 'school'. Harry had tried everything to stop his friend from leaving: racing round his cage, showing off his best **POPCORNING** acrobatics or making the rumbly purring noise that always made Billy smile. But nothing worked: not even his most ear-splitting **WHEEKS**. It seemed that Billy had no choice in the matter. Harry longed to go with him and now, finally, it seemed that he actually would. Yes, Harry Stevenson was going to school!

Harry chewed on a strand of hay and thought about 'school'. *What will it be like?* he wondered. He'd heard a lot of things from Billy: some bad, some good. Depending on how Billy was feeling, school either sounded like a boring, cramped hutch, or a big outdoor run with lots of grass and dandelions. Harry was sure that it would be like the outdoor run today, with extra dandelions. He couldn't wait to find out! There was going to be so much to see: strange things called 'classrooms', 'teachers' and 'uniform' (although apparently Harry wouldn't be wearing that). And what about 'maths'? Harry chattered his teeth with disapproval. From the fuss Billy made about maths homework, it sounded very unpleasant – possibly even dangerous. Harry hoped he wouldn't come across any maths at school.

Just as Harry chomped down the last of the hay strand and was about to select another, Billy came into the room.

'Hey, Harry,' said Billy, gathering up his friend and walking into the kitchen. Harry snuggled into Billy's arms and sighed with happiness. It was breakfast time! Breakfast had always been exciting for Harry, but now it was extra special because he got to enjoy it with the Smiths rather than in his cage. Billy had been given a plastic pet carrier for his birthday and this had become Harry's place at (or rather on) the kitchen table. There wasn't much

room between the boxes of cereal, jam jars, newspapers, bills, piles of washed socks and school books, but the carrier just about fitted. Harry loved to sit there, ideally with a spinach leaf or two, and poke his nose out of the door so he could keep an eye on the family as they ate. As usual, he sniffed the air to check there was nothing on their plates he could **WHEEK** for – and hopefully share – but today all he could smell was toast and marmalade.

Mr Smith spotted Harry's eager face peeping from the carrier and winked. 'Nothing for you here, Greedy,' he smiled.

How rude! thought Harry. But then he remembered that this was a Very Special Day and decided not to mind.

'I can't believe Harry Stevenson's coming to school today!' said Billy, slathering butter on his toast.

I can't either, thought Harry. *Yippee!*

'Are you *sure* it's OK to take Harry to school, Billy?' asked Mrs Smith, looking worried.

'I've told you, Mum!' said Billy. 'Miss Gibby asked us to bring in our favourite thing for a special Show and Tell. Harry's *definitely* my favourite thing . . . aren't you, Harry?'

'Hmmm,' said Mrs Smith. 'I think she might have meant something less fluffy. Or squeaky.'

'It'll be fine, love!' said Mr Smith. 'Harry's only small. He won't be any trouble at all.'

Harry crouched down in the hay and did his best impression of an innocent, trouble-free pet, while Mrs Smith gave him a long, hard stare.

'I'm not convinced,' she said. 'That guinea pig turns trouble into an art form.

And, speaking of art, isn't the painting competition being judged today?'

Billy nodded. 'Yes, Mum, it's this afternoon. Can you guess what I painted?'

Mrs Smith smiled. 'Hmm, Billy, I wonder. Was it small and furry by any chance? With a squeaky voice and a massive appetite?'

Billy looked surprised. 'Er, yes, Mum. I painted Harry. How did you know?!'

Mrs Smith knows everything, thought Harry admiringly. He wondered why she and Mr Smith were laughing, though.

CHAPTER 2

Off to school,
Harry Stevenson?

Soon it was time to leave. Harry watched impatiently from his carrier as the Smiths bustled about, getting their belongings together. As usual, there was some last-minute faffing while Billy looked for his homework and then tried to find a shoe. (If Harry could talk Human, he would have

said, 'Hurry up, Billy, it's under the sofa!')
Just like every other day, Mrs Smith got a
bit shirty and rolled her eyes, and of course
Mr Smith had forgotten where he'd put the
keys to his van, just as he always did. But
one thing was different as the Smith family
FINALLY tumbled out of the door in a big
noisy jumble – Harry was going with them!

'WHEEK, WHEEK, WHEEK!' cried
Harry in excitement as the Smiths hurried
down the garden path. Why didn't Billy
feel this excited about going to school? he
wondered. *If I was Billy*, thought Harry, *I'd be
skipping down that path each day, singing
my happiest song at the top of my voice.*

Harry peered out from the carrier to watch

Mrs Smith head off to catch the bus that would take her to work, then Mr Smith and Billy climbed into the van. Harry looked around. The van had not got any cleaner since its debut on the Sparky FC pitch – in fact, it looked even grubbier, if that was possible. Harry didn't care – he couldn't wait to get to school so as long as the van started, it could look as messy as it liked!

As Billy settled Harry's carrier on his lap, its door swung open slightly.

'That door looks loose, son,' said Mr Smith. 'Just keep an eye on it and I'll fix it later.'

'Thanks, Dad,' said Billy, carefully fastening it shut. 'Ooh, there's Maya!'

Harry watched as the Smiths' neighbour, Maya Matthews, got into the van. Maya was the same age as Billy and, after a shaky start, the pair were now good friends. Maya's mum, Mrs Matthews, was a police officer and Maya's dog Mack worked for the police too. They'd been very busy lately as there had been a lot of robberies in the city over the past few weeks. Mrs Matthews and Mack were working a long shift today so Maya needed a lift to school.

'Everyone ready, then?' said Mr Smith. 'Right, let's go.' With a mighty backfire and a puff of black smoke, the van started up. *Phew!* thought Harry as it trundled down the street. *We're off!* Mr Smith whistled happily as he drove and Harry felt so content that he couldn't help but join in – this was going to be an excellent day!

Snug in the carrier perched on Billy's lap, Harry Stevenson had a good view out of the window. He looked around eagerly, his hungry eyes taking everything in. It was rush hour and the streets were busy with life. Harry saw lots of children and their parents waiting at bus stops. It was interesting to see the children's uniforms change as the van passed through different areas – he spotted black, grey, blue, green, red and even yellow school jumpers. Harry recalled how big the city had looked from the air and shuddered as he remembered his balloon-powered solo flight – seeing the world from the van was much more enjoyable.

Every now and again, Billy and Maya would point things out to Harry. Billy showed him his favourite newsagent's, which had an amazing selection of sweets and stickers, and Maya pointed to the pet shop where the Matthews bought dog treats for Mack. Harry's eyes sparkled with excitement when Maya described the products for guinea pigs sold there – chewy tubes, crunchy snacks and special hay that was full of meadow flowers. *What a place!* he thought.

'Nearly there, Harry!' said Billy, and Harry Stevenson danced in the hay with excitement. He wriggled and jiggled, tip-tapped his toes and nibbled a few nuggets, but nothing could calm him down. He decided to give himself another wash in order to look as smart as possible. As Harry carefully cleaned his fur, he listened to Billy and Maya talking about Show and Tell. It was part of a big project the school was running called 'My Favourite Thing'. The art competition was part of that too, and other schools across the country were taking part. Maya had wanted to bring Mack the dog as *he* was her favourite thing, but poor Mack was too busy at work. So instead Maya had brought her Sparky FC league winners' medal.

At long last the journey was over. Harry gave himself one last brush-down and combed out his whiskers with his paws. 'Here we are, kiddos,' said Mr Smith, sliding open the doors and helping the children out of the van. 'Have a great day, Maya. You mind that guinea pig, Billy. And as for you, you greedy little hog – make sure you behave yourself!'

But the greedy little hog wasn't listening – he was staring out of his carrier, open-mouthed with awe. For there in front of Harry, towering up into the sky (well, to some medium-sized treetops at least), was a big

red-brick building with a brightly coloured sign over its gates, high windows decorated with flags and pictures, and a playground filled with hundreds of children.

School! thought Harry Stevenson.

CHAPTER 3

King of the playground, Harry Stevenson

Harry Stevenson had watched a lot of films on the sofa with Billy, and in one of them the heroes walked into town in slow motion, striding along like they owned the street and looking very cool indeed. It felt *a lot* like that to Harry as Billy and Maya passed through the school gates and went into the playground. Harry's heart raced with joy as he took in the scene. There was a lot to see. Hordes of children were running around in a laughing, shouting, whizzing blur of colour. There were footballs and skipping ropes, wild shrieking games of chase, and all sorts of general charging-about going on.

So this *is school*, thought Harry. His first impression was: *School is busy*. And his second was: *School is* very *noisy!* It was all quite overwhelming. But then he heard Billy calling out to his friends, and Jake and Daniel came running up. Harry had met them both at Billy's party and it was reassuring to see familiar faces.

'Hey, Billy, hey, Maya!' said Jake. 'And, oh! Hey, Harry!'

There were more footsteps as Jess and Scarlett came over to join them.

'Hi, everyone!' they called. 'Wow, Billy, you really have brought Harry. HELLO, HARRY!'

'Cool, a guinea pig!' said a girl nearby, and before long Harry was in the middle of a big circle of children, all oohing and aahing over him, and telling Billy how much they wished *they* had a guinea pig too. Harry Stevenson shook his whiskers with pride. Billy was part of a group now and, excitingly, so was Harry!

Harry felt like the king of the playground

as the friends walked over to their favourite bench. They started talking about Show and Tell, and soon were laughing out loud as they'd ALL (apart from Billy) brought their Sparky FC medals.

'Uh-oh!' said Jake. 'There goes Jack.' Harry looked up. He'd heard all about Jack from Billy. Jack was a friendly boy, but he *did* like playing jokes. Sometimes they went a bit too far, Harry knew – like that time with the earwig in the sandwich. (The earwig had turned out to be plastic, which was lucky for all concerned, especially the earwig.) *Everyone* had had a Jack joke played on them at some point, Billy's friends said. As a new boy, it was only a matter of time before it happened to Billy and Harry didn't like the sound of that at all.

'There's Miss Gibby!' said Billy. Harry peered out curiously. Miss Gibby was Billy's teacher so he often talked about her. Harry knew that she was kind and funny, but could be strict, and that she was a big fan of Sparky FC. Billy said that there was even a picture of the team above her desk! Harry had always wondered what Miss Gibby looked like. He could see a lady with sleek fair hair, wearing a brightly patterned dress. Miss Gibby had a kind but nervous face. She seemed a lot younger than Mr and Mrs Smith, and was carrying a shiny bell with a wooden handle.

'I'm hiding Harry from Miss Gibby,' Billy said, picking up the carrier so its wire front faced his chest and couldn't be seen. 'I want her to have a **REALLY BIG SURPRISE** when we do Show and Tell.'

Never mind Miss Gibby – it was **HARRY** who got a really big surprise just then because, at that moment, she loudly rang the bell: **CLANG, CLANG, CLANG!** Harry jumped so far in the air that he bumped his head on the carrier roof: *Oof!*

The circles of chattering, giggling children broke up, and came together again in giggly, chatty lines in front of their teachers. When Billy joined the back of Miss Gibby's line, he found himself next to a boy who was carrying a cardboard box very carefully. Harry felt a chill of fear when he saw that box – there was something about it that made him uneasy.

'Hi, Fergus,' said Billy. 'What's in your box?'

But he never got to find out because Miss Gibby called for quiet. Then she turned and led her class into the school building. Harry Stevenson peeped out from the carrier and took in the view. Everything about school felt a LOT bigger than the Smiths' flat, so he was glad to be safe inside the carrier. Harry wondered if he was the very first guinea pig ever to set paw in the school, just like those astronauts on the moon in a film he'd watched with Billy.

The line of children snaked into the main building, past a friendly-looking lady on the reception desk, turned a corner and then went up, up, up a twisting staircase. All the walls were covered in paintings, drawings and photographs. Harry tried to spot Billy in the pictures, but they were moving too fast.

After what seemed to Harry like a lot of stairs, corners, corridors and doors, the long procession ended. The children streamed into their classroom and went to sit at low wooden tables. Billy headed for one at the back of the class and put the carrier down on the tabletop, its door facing away from Miss Gibby again. He didn't want to spoil the surprise!

'Are you OK, Harry?' Billy whispered. Harry couldn't answer, of course, but he was more than OK – he was enthralled! Snug in the hay, he had a perfect view of the classroom through the holes in the carrier. Harry could see all the children's backs, and Miss Gibby sitting at her desk at the front of the class, next to a whiteboard on the wall. He could also see Fergus's box underneath a table nearby. As he stared at the box, it seemed to move a little. Harry blinked. No, he must have imagined it. But there was *definitely* something sinister about that box.

'Good morning, class 3G,' said Miss Gibby.

'Good **MOR-NING, MISS GI-BBY!'** chanted the children happily. 'Good **MOR-NING, EVERY-BO-DY!'**

'Well!' said Miss Gibby. 'What an exciting day this is! It's our Show and Tell, but there's something else happening too.'

'*Oooooooooooh!*' sang the class.

'What you *did* know is that today our art competition will be judged,' continued Miss

Gibby. 'But what you *didn't* know is that we have some **VERY SPECIAL** visitors coming in to do it: the city mayor, a reporter and a professional artist. Now you know what I'm going to say, don't you? I want everyone to promise to be on their VERY BEST BEHAVIOUR!'

'WE PRO-MISE, MISS GI-BBY!' chorused the class.

Harry Stevenson almost joined in with a noisy squeak, but remembered just in time that he was supposed to be a **REALLY BIG SURPRISE.** *They seem like* very *well-behaved children*, Harry thought. Then he noticed that one of the boys had his fingers crossed behind his back. Harry looked closer – it was Jack.

Crossed fingers – *what does THAT mean?* wondered Harry.

CHAPTER 4

Good morning, Harry Stevenson

Miss Gibby took the register and Harry felt a thrill of pride when she read out Billy's name. Then she announced it was time for Show and Tell. Harry listened carefully. He wanted to be a perfect pupil today; if he was very good, perhaps Miss Gibby would give him a sticker, or even a merit mark.

Miss Gibby started to talk about Favourite Things. *Her* Favourite Things, she said, were strawberries and sunshine (Harry nodded approvingly) – but what about the class? It was time to find out. Harry watched as one by one the children got up to Show and Tell.

They had brought *all sorts* of interesting things:

A sparkly snow globe from New York.

A saxophone.

A scruffy, saggy old cuddly bear.

A tiny metal cannon that was also a pencil sharpener.

A plastic unicorn with a rainbow mane and glittery wings.

And one, two, three, four, FIVE Sparky FC medals!

Soon there were only two more pupils to Show and Tell: Billy and Fergus.

'Who's going first, boys?' asked Miss Gibby. Harry couldn't wait to be shown off, so he was very pleased when he heard Billy call out.

'Me, please, Miss Gibby!' begged Billy, jiggling around in his seat and holding his arm high in the air.

'All right then, Billy,' she laughed. 'You're obviously keen to get going. What have you brought to show us?'

Billy got up to speak. He patted down his

hair. He cleared his throat. Then he cleared it again: *Ahem*. Everyone, including Harry Stevenson, waited for Billy to start. But nothing happened. Poor Billy was getting redder and redder, and looking more and more unhappy. *Oh no*, thought Harry, *Billy's got stage fright!*

'Don't worry, Billy,' said Miss Gibby kindly. 'Let's play a game. Why don't you give us some clues and we'll try to guess what you've brought? It might be fun! Does that sound OK to you?'

Billy nodded and looked a bit happier.

'Um, OK,' he mumbled. 'Well, what I've brought is *furry*.'

'A teddy bear!' cried the children.

'A stuffed squirrel!' shouted Jack, who could always be relied on to say something unusual.

'Erm, no,' croaked Billy, a bit louder this time. 'Not a bear or a squirrel. It makes A LOT OF NOISE.'

'It's a tambourine!'

'A recorder!'

'A kazoo!'

Billy smiled. 'No, it's not those either. It's *very* funny,' he said, 'and it makes me laugh every day.'

'Is it a joke book?' asked Fergus.

'It's a **FURRY WHOOPEE CUSHION!**' called Jack.

Everyone laughed at this, and so did Billy.

Phew! thought Harry Stevenson. *He's going to be all right.*

'No,' continued Billy, 'it's nothing like that. Well, maybe a bit . . .' He thought for a while and then all his words tumbled out in a rush. 'It's not an "it" though – it's a "he". He's small and squeaky and he lives with me and my mum and dad. He's really cool . . . and, and he's my best friend in the whole world.'

It was impossible to see under all that ginger fur, but Harry Stevenson was blushing like mad as Billy brought him out of the carrier and lifted him up to show the class. *Funny . . . cool . . . Billy's best friend!* Hearing those words was one of the happiest moments in Harry's life.

'OOOOOOHHHHHHHH, Harry Stevenson!' gasped the class and everyone stood up for a better look. Harry realized that Billy must have talked about him because all the children knew his name, and he blushed even more.

Miss Gibby had certainly had a **REALLY BIG SURPRISE**. For a while, she stood there, speechless.

'My goodness!' she said eventually. 'A **GUINEA PIG!** That's not QUITE what I had in mind, Billy.' She sighed. 'Well, I suppose he's here now . . .'

All of a sudden Harry felt terrible. Miss Gibby wasn't happy that he was here! His whiskers drooped with sadness as he buried his face in Billy's arms. The Very Special Day had gone wrong! Then he felt someone stroking his fur and it didn't feel like Billy's touch. Harry turned his head round to see Miss Gibby staring at him thoughtfully. She stroked his fur again. Harry nuzzled her finger with his nose.

'Hmmm,' Miss Gibby said. 'You're certainly a charmer, Harry Stevenson.'

Harry gave her finger another nuzzle, and then a friendly lick for good measure. Miss Gibby smiled.

'Well, Harry Stevenson,' she said, 'I've never met a guinea pig before, but if they're all like you I think I like them. You may as well stay for the day; just behave yourself, mind.'

Miss Gibby turned to the class. 'Children, I'd like you to welcome a new member of 3G: Harry Stevenson!'

The children cheered and sung out their welcome.

'GOOD MOR-NING, HAR-EE STEE-VEN-SON!'

CHAPTER 5

What's in the box, Harry Stevenson?

Now it was Fergus's turn to Show and Tell. Harry sat on Billy's lap and watched as Fergus picked up his cardboard box and placed it on a table. Harry had a very bad feeling about that box. It might have looked like a boring cardboard box to you and me, but to Harry it was a MENACING BOX

OF DREAD. It must have been his ancient guinea-pig instinct kicking in! Harry knew that being scared of unfamiliar things and sensing danger *everywhere* was simply the Way of the Guinea Pig. (Running like mad when necessary was too.) It was how his ancestors had survived in the wild. The Smiths' back garden was about as wild as Harry's life got, but the need to hide, watch and flee ran deep inside him. *I've seen the nature programmes*, he thought. *You can't be too careful if you're small and fluffy.*

So Harry watched with a rising feeling of terror as Fergus rummaged inside the box. And then, horror of horrors, Fergus pulled out something **SO SCARY** Harry's whiskers nearly froze off with fear. For there in Fergus's arms, looking out at the class with what to Harry seemed like a *seriously* evil stare, was a

DREADFUL,
FEARSOME,
PETRIFYING . . .
. . . SNAKE!!!!!!

'YIKES!' yelped half the children (and Miss Gibby), drawing back as far as they could from Fergus.

'*C O O L !*' breathed the other half, leaning forward to get a better look.

You can guess which half Harry was in. He felt like he was going to faint! He wriggled as close as he could to Billy, who could sense his friend's fear and picked him up to protect him. Harry whickered gratefully: Billy was so kind.

'This is Flash,' said Fergus proudly. 'He's a corn snake. He's very gentle and he's really sleepy as he had a big breakfast this morning. He's very easy to keep, he's super-clever and I think he's the BEST PET EVER.'

Best pet ever? huffed Harry Stevenson, feeling a lot braver now he was safe in Billy's arms. *Can Flash popcorn, or* **WHEEK,** *or make rumbly noises?* I DON'T THINK SO! *And he's not exactly cuddly either!*

Harry felt even more jealous when he saw that lots of the children were gathering round Fergus for a closer look at his snake. Someone asked what Flash ate, and Harry covered his ears with his paws – he didn't want to think about that. UGH!!!

Harry wasn't going to have ANYTHING to do with that creature. No, thank you! Sleepy or not, a snake was no friend to a guinea pig.

It took a while for Miss Gibby to calm her class down. She looked as if she needed calming down herself. She had turned very pale and her hair wasn't looking quite so sleek. It had gone a bit frizzy and she kept patting it flat. Flash and Harry were put back in their carriers, but the children were overexcited by the snake's presence: either pretending to be more scared than they really were, or showing off that they weren't scared at all. Harry could see one boy standing on a chair and refusing to come down, while another girl was slithering her hands up and down a classmate's back, pretending to be a snake. (The classmate was not happy about this and was pointing it out at the top of his voice.) Just then there was a knock on the door. Miss Gibby looked up and went even paler as it opened.

'It's Mrs Edwards, the headteacher!' Billy whispered to Harry.

Uh-oh! thought Harry. Billy had told him that Mrs Edwards was Very Strict Indeed. There were three other people with the head – a friendly-looking woman wearing an enormous gold chain, a serious-faced man with a beard and a beret, and a rather scary-looking woman clutching a notebook.

From his carrier, Harry studied them and wondered who they were. By the looks of it, none of the class knew either.

'Good morning, Miss Gibby. Good morning, 3G,' said Mrs Edwards.

'*Good mor-ning, Mrs Ed-wards*,' chanted the children.

'This is Mrs Singh, the mayor, Mr Dunn, an artist, and Mrs Finch, a reporter from the *City News*,' said Mrs Edwards. 'They've

kindly come to judge our art competition today, and I'm showing them round the school. Miss Gibby, we heard some rather strange noises coming from your classroom. Is everything all right?'

'Yes, it was just a bit of . . . erm . . . natural history!' blushed Miss Gibby, who didn't want to admit to having not only a guinea pig in her classroom, but a real live snake too. It's probably not a situation that *any* teacher would want to deal with – just ask yours at school!

'Yes,' she went on. 'We were having a science lesson. The children were learning about, um . . . zoology.'

'Zoology?!' said the reporter, raising her

eyebrows and scribbling in her notebook. 'Well, that *is* different.'

Miss Gibby blushed even more and smoothed her hair down, but it bounced back wilder than before.

Poor Miss Gibby, thought Harry, and glared at the visitors for making her nervous.

'I thought your class started with maths today,' said Mrs Edwards.

Miss Gibby swallowed and cleared her throat.

'Maths?' she croaked. 'Oh, yes. Yes, that's right. We're just getting ready for maths!'

'I'm very glad to hear it, Miss Gibby,' said Mrs Edwards as she and the visitors left the room.

Phew, thought Harry Stevenson, relieved that no one had spotted him. But wait. Had Miss Gibby just said . . . maths? Now *Harry* felt nervous too!

CHAPTER 6

Learn your sums, Harry Stevenson!

Harry Stevenson still had no idea what maths actually was, but, from the sighs and moans coming from the class, his worst fears were confirmed. Maths *had* to be something **REALLY** nasty. So Harry was surprised when Miss Gibby asked Billy if he and Harry could help with the lesson – and even more so when Billy said yes!

'Put Harry down here, Billy,' said Miss Gibby, pointing to her desk.

What's going on? thought Harry as Billy carried him to the front of the class. *When will the maths start?*

Now he was sitting on Miss Gibby's desk, Harry could see all the children's faces. Everyone was gazing at him happily, but, instead of looking back, Harry's eyes were drawn to the corner where Flash's box had been placed. Harry shuddered as he thought of the snake inside. Luckily, his attention was diverted by a rustling noise – Miss Gibby was rummaging in a shopping bag. Harry couldn't help making a very loud

WHEEK – the rustling of plastic meant only one thing to this guinea pig: food.

And Harry was right! To his delight, he could see Miss Gibby open up a bag of mini carrots. He popcorned with happiness; those carrots looked tasty. The class giggled.

'These were for my lunch,' said Miss Gibby, 'but the dinner ladies have made my favourite pie. I think I'll use them for our maths lesson instead.'

Harry was puzzled – what did carrots have to do with maths?

Miss Gibby placed some of the carrots beside him, before turning away to write on the board. 'So,' she said as she wrote out a sum, 'if Harry has three carrots and I give him four more . . . how many carrots does Harry have?'

Would *you* be able to give Miss Gibby the right answer? It seemed that no one in 3G could! Harry looked out at a sea of hands in the air – all the children were desperate to answer – but everyone got it wrong. Miss Gibby sounded crosser and crosser.

'*Six!*' called a voice from the back.

'Good try, Daniel, but that's not quite right.'

'Five!' cried another voice.

'Now come on, class. I know you know the answer.'

'Four and a half!'

'Jemima, we're not doing fractions this term.'

'Four!'

Miss Gibby got more and more worked up as the children kept calling out the wrong number, getting lower each time: *'Three and a half,'* then *'Three,'* then *'Two!'* A few of the children were trying not to laugh, which made poor Miss Gibby even more flustered. Meanwhile, Billy was hopping up and down beside her, going pink in the face trying to attract her attention without interrupting too much. But Miss Gibby ignored him and kept her focus on the class.

'Let everyone else have a chance, Billy,' she said.

Shiver my whiskers! Maths is HARD, thought Harry. No wonder Billy got so worked up about his homework.

Finally, Billy looked as if he was about to burst. He yelled out: 'MISS GIBBY, MISS GIBBY, MISS GIBBY!'

Miss Gibby turned round in surprise. Billy pointed to her desk and she followed his gaze to where Harry sat. *Oops*, thought Harry, looking up guiltily as the classroom went quiet. It wasn't *entirely* silent though. There was one small noise to be heard: a chomping, chewing, lip-smacking sort of noise. It was the sound of a guinea pig hurriedly scoffing down the last remaining mini carrot. You see, Harry had been doing his own version of 'maths' – subtraction!

Miss Gibby clapped her hand to her head and gave a very deep sigh.

It was all too much for the children – the giggles they'd managed to hold back as Harry wolfed down the carrots started to bubble out. First someone snorted, then someone else sniggered, the pupil next to them chortled, and soon the whole class was roaring with laughter.

As he brushed the last delicious orange morsels from his fur, Harry heard Miss Gibby mutter, 'Could this day get any worse?'

Oh dear. Apparently it could. For

peering in through the glass window of the classroom door, and looking mightily suspicious as she did so, was Mrs Edwards, the headteacher, with her Very Important Guests.

Mrs Edwards opened the door and came in.

'Miss Gibby, are you *quite* all right?' she demanded. 'Your classroom seems awfully noisy today.'

'All fine here!' said Miss Gibby hurriedly, standing in front of Harry in an attempt to keep him hidden. 'We were, er, just doing a little drama.'

'Drama?!' snapped Mrs Edwards. 'I thought you were doing maths?'

'Zoology and drama too!' said Mrs Finch the reporter. 'You certainly have a unique approach, Miss Gibby.' And she scribbled furiously in her notebook. Mrs Edwards looked cross.

I don't think the head likes zoology or drama, whatever THEY are, mused Harry.

Harry thought that Miss Gibby seemed *very* relieved when the head and her guests left the classroom. She slumped in her chair and patted down her hair. By now it was looking very messy. It reminded Harry of a pile of hay, which made him feel hungry all over again.

'Breaktime!' called Miss Gibby weakly. 'Everyone go and have a run around. And,

Billy and Fergus, DO make sure your pets are safe and secure, please.'

Safe and secure sounds good to me, thought Harry Stevenson once he was back in his carrier. He gave Flash's box his sternest stare. Luckily, it had been moved to the far side of the classroom, otherwise Harry would not have felt quite so brave. *I'll keep an eye on things and sound the alarm if there are any problems*, vowed Harry, still hoping for a sticker or a merit award.

He settled down into the hay and prepared for lookout duty. *My whiskers, maths tasted good*, he thought with a yawn. *Those little carrots were exceptionally tasty!* Harry yawned again – he always felt dozy after eating, and maths had turned into a hefty snack. Soon Harry nodded off. It was tiring stuff, this 'school' business.

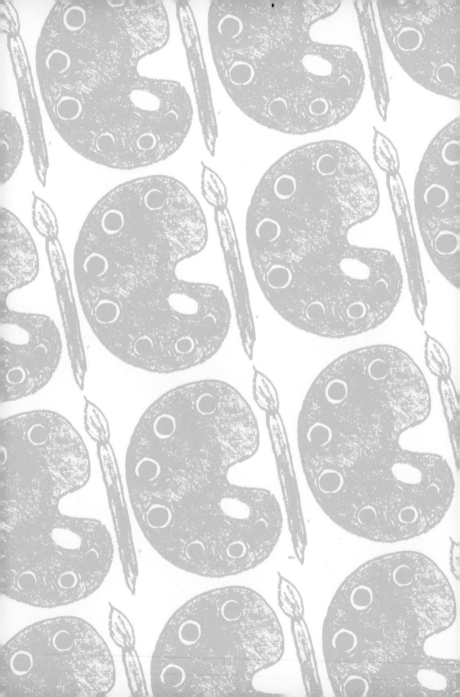

CHAPTER 7

Don't do it,
Harry Stevenson

Harry Stevenson was woken by the sound of footsteps. He lay groggily in the hay at the back of his carrier. The footsteps moved across the classroom, stopped for a bit, and then went back the way they'd come. What was going on? Harry crept to the front of the carrier so he could look out. It was

Jack! Just as the boy was leaving the room, he bumped into Miss Gibby.

'Is everything all right, Jack?' she asked.

'Er, it's fine, Miss,' said Jack as he ducked past her through the door. 'I forgot my bag, that's all.'

Hmmm, thought Harry, his guinea-pig instinct flashing a warning. *Something's not quite right here. I can feel it in my whiskers.* He knew from Billy that Jack could be naughty – what *was* he up to?

Miss Gibby set to work getting the room

ready for the next lesson: art. Harry watched as she put up a long line of wooden easels, then laid out paints, water bowls and mixing palettes. Finally, she placed a pile of blank canvasses at the side of the room for the children to choose from. Miss Gibby hummed as she worked. She seemed a lot happier than before. *Perhaps Miss Gibby doesn't like maths very much*, thought Harry.

Finally, Miss Gibby's work was done and she left the room. It felt very empty and still without any humans around. The only noise came from a tick-tocking clock on the wall. Harry lounged in the hay, keeping a careful eye on Flash's box. He watched it for several minutes, but there was no movement or sound. *That snake must be asleep*, he thought.

Harry Stevenson started to feel a little bit bored and *very* hungry. He'd eaten all his vegetables and nuggets hours ago. They were supposed to last all day, but Harry wasn't very good at making food last. *There must be something else to eat*, he thought. He nosed around the carrier, sniffing through the hay for fragments of leftover carrots or nuggets. Nothing. Soon the ticks of the clock were joined by a deeper sound: Harry's growling stomach.

Then Harry remembered Miss Gibby's bag. *There were carrots in there before, so perhaps there are carrots in there now*, reasoned Harry. He closed his eyes, remembering that sweet, tasty crunch. *Mmmmm, lovely orange carrots*, he thought dreamily.

Harry peeped out to check if the bag was still under Miss Gibby's desk: yes, there it was.

And that was it. Once Harry Stevenson had sniffed out even the *merest possibility* of a carrot, he couldn't stop himself. Remembering that the door to his carrier was loose, Harry pushed it open and stepped out. He quickly scanned the room. The quickest route to Miss Gibby's bag took him past Flash's box: that was no good. Harry would need to venture across the middle of the classroom to avoid it.

Like a tiny ginger ninja, Harry darted silently under the tables, scurrying from schoolbag to schoolbag and crouching

down each time to hide. Soon he reached the shopping bag and peered in. *YES!* There were still a couple of carrots inside. Harry had just settled down to feast on them when he heard a most unusual sound.

SSSSSSSSSSSSSSS . . .

Harry looked up but saw nothing. *Strange* . . . He turned back to the carrots, impatient to finish them.

SSSSSSSSSSSSSSSS.

Well, that really *was* an unusual sound – but not unfamiliar. *Now where have I heard that noise before?* pondered Harry, his mind focused mainly on carrots. *Hmmm. It was on TV, wasn't it?* He thought harder as his carrot-fog cleared. *Some kind of nature programme maybe? About jungles perhaps . . . with possibly even a reptile or two?*

Oh dear.

SSSSSSSSSSS!!!!!

Harry Stevenson looked up in horror – straight into a pair of cold pale eyes that were coming at him in a slithery, speedy and positively snake-like fashion.

Yikes! thought Harry Stevenson as Flash the corn snake shot towards him.

RUN!!

CHAPTER 8

Quick,
Harry Stevenson!

Harry Stevenson ran like the clappers. It was the Way of the Guinea Pig. He didn't even have to think about it – his little legs just worked by themselves.

As Harry scurried hither and thither across the classroom, Flash slithered close behind. The snake could move fast, so Harry had to be clever. He jumped from schoolbag to schoolbag, hoping to confuse his foe. But Flash wasn't fooled: just like Fergus said, he was super-clever. Harry couldn't shake him off.

Harry decided that the only way to outpace Flash was to get off the floor and find somewhere safe. He wasn't sure if corn snakes could climb, but it was worth a try. The tables and chairs were too high for a little creature like Harry to jump on to in one go so he needed a launch pad. Looking urgently ahead, Harry spotted a line of schoolbags at the side of the classroom. If he could clamber on top of them, he could jump on to a chair, and from there on to a table. Harry raced towards the schoolbags and scampered up the side of the smallest one. Then he clambered up each bag until he'd reached the tallest – but Flash was still following!

Harry took a deep breath, closed his eyes and flung himself from the tallest bag in a great big squeaky leap.

'WHEEEKKKKK!!!' he cried. He landed on a chair with a bump and looked back. Flash seemed confused, weaving his head to and fro, his tongue flicking in the air. Perhaps he couldn't jump? But the snake simply slithered back down the bags, across the floor and over to Harry's chair!

'**WHEEEK!!!!**' wheeked Harry again, making another jump from the chair to the table. *Surely I'm safe here*, he thought. But no, Flash had climbed up on to the table too! Harry sped round it, pursued by Flash, with both guinea pig and snake knocking over paint pots and jam jars filled with water as they went. Things got very slippery for the pair of them, and at one point Harry slid and fell. *This is it!* he thought in panic,

his feet scrabbling in blue paint. But Flash was skidding around too, so Harry had time to get up and flee.

But there was nowhere to run! Flash had Harry cornered by the edge of the table. *Here I go again*, thought Harry Stevenson, taking another HUGE LEAP and aiming for the next table. **'WHEEEEKKKKKKKK!!!!'** he yelled, zooming through the air and making a very bumpy landing. His feet were still slippery with paint, and the force

of Harry's jump made him skid across the table straight on to a mixing palette of red and yellow paint!

WHOOSH!! The palette whizzed across the table and off the other side. Harry rode that palette like a snowboard as it flew gracefully through the air, then landed on the floor. It continued to slide across the classroom, leaving a trail of colour in its wake.

CRASH!!! The palette hit a wall and splashed more paint everywhere. Covered in red and yellow paint, Harry flew into the air and landed **SPLAT** on top of the pile of canvasses. *OOF!* He rolled over and over, before scrabbling to his feet and staggering around in a daze.

Oh dear.

As Harry looked up, he spotted two things. Neither was a sight to make him feel happy.

The first was Flash shooting at high speed across the classroom after losing control on the slippery tabletops. The snake had no feet to act as brakes, so, just like Harry's mixing palette, he hurtled across the tables, getting faster and faster as he went, then rocketed into the air. The hapless snake flew slap into the side of an easel with an almighty **SMACK**.

Ouch, winced Harry Stevenson as Flash fell to the floor. *That must have REALLY hurt.* The snake lay winded for a few seconds, and then slowly, wearily and wonkily, slunk off to hide in his box. It's hard to spot emotion on the face of a snake, but Harry could have sworn that Flash looked embarrassed.

The second sight was even worse. There in the doorway stood an appalled Miss Gibby and her class, staring open-mouthed at the classroom. A classroom that, Harry realized as he looked around in horror, had been turned into a scene of complete devastation. There were upturned chairs all

over the place, great puddles of water on the floor and splashes of paint dripping down the walls. It was as if a gang of rainbows had had a massive fight in 3G's classroom. Harry looked down at his paws and saw that he too was multicoloured. He was no longer ginger, but a stripey, splodgy, technicolour rodent.

And that wasn't all.

A sudden creaking sound made everyone turn towards the easel that Flash had crashed into. It had been rocking back and forth from the force of the blow, and now, ever so gently, it started to tip over.

Please, no, thought Harry Stevenson as he watched the easel fall slowly . . . on to

the next in line. The second easel wobbled
a bit, then it too toppled over, knocking
into the one beside it, and, like a line
of dominoes, every single easel sent its
neighbour crashing noisily to the floor.
BANG! SMASH!

When the dust settled, Harry peered up

at Miss Gibby from his puddle of paint. Someone else was here too: Mrs Edwards the head. Harry gulped.

From the look on everyone's faces, he knew this was very, *very* bad.

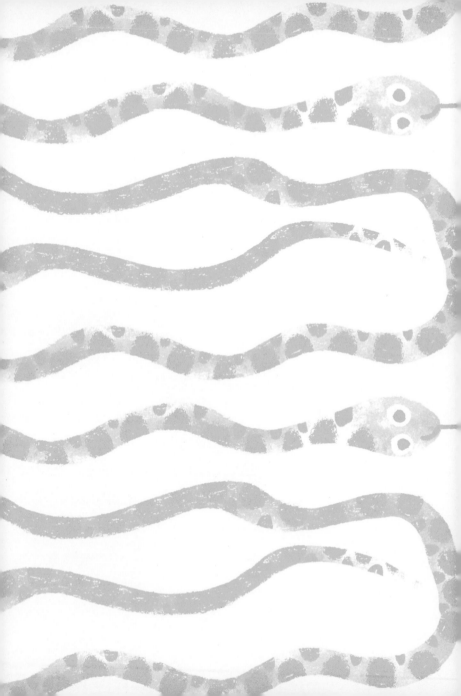

CHAPTER 9

Oh,
Harry Stevenson...

The children set to work to clean up the mess that Harry Stevenson, and his eternal quest for carrots, had caused. They put the easels back up, mopped up the spilled water and tried to scrub away the paint. It didn't all come off though – it was going to take a lot of work to remove . . . Even though it hadn't been *entirely* his fault, Harry felt terrible.

Harry wasn't the only one to feel guilty – Jack had been shocked by what had happened, and said sorry to Billy and Fergus, and Harry too! Jack explained that he'd just thought it would be funny to let Flash have the run of the classroom. He'd never expected Harry to be out of his cage as well.

Harry sighed. *If only I'd stayed in the carrier, none of this would have happened*, he thought.

Poor Miss Gibby picked up the canvas that Harry had landed on. It was covered in red and yellow splodges, which in places merged into smudges of orange. There were also some scrabbly pawprints, which had scuffed up the paint marks even more. It was ruined. Miss Gibby sighed and leaned it against the art chest to dry. She had been a teacher for a long time, but she'd never had a day like this.

Harry needed cleaning too, so Billy gave him a wash in the classroom sink. Miss Gibby said that everyone could watch, so long as they didn't crowd in and frighten Harry. Harry *never* liked having a wash and he always made a big fuss, even though Billy was always gentle and careful. Having one in public was even worse! Harry **SQUEAKED** like mad in protest as Billy slowly poured a dribble of warm water over him, which ran off him in vivid colours. Squeaking was no use though: Billy just carried on. It took a few goes, but eventually Harry was ginger

again. Billy wrapped Harry up in an old school jumper and he peered out crossly. He looked so sweet and bedraggled in his 'school uniform' that everyone laughed.

Hmph! thought Harry Stevenson. *If it cheers everyone up, then I suppose the bath was worth it.* Even Miss Gibby smiled, although Harry thought she still looked pale.

'Come on, 3G,' she said. 'Let's forget about the mess for now. It's nearly time for the judging of the art competition so we need to get ready!'

The class happily collected their pictures from the art chest. Harry was back in his carrier by now, but lots of the children brought their pictures over to show him. He was very impressed! Jake and Daniel had both done pictures of Sparky FC: Jake had painted the Sparky logo, while Daniel's picture showed a football slamming into the net of a goal. Jess had come up with a still-life of apples, and Scarlett had made a big, swirly drawing of spaghetti! She'd taken her pencil and whirled it round and round the paper. Maya had used felt-tip pens to draw a portrait of Mack looking fierce and proud. He really did look

noble. Harry admired the picture and wished his doggy friend could visit school too.

When Harry Stevenson saw Billy's picture he could have popped with happiness. Billy had used hundreds of tiny orange brushstrokes to paint a picture of Harry. There were two glossy black painted dots for eyes, and Billy had carefully drawn his friend's nose, mouth and whiskers with a pencil. Billy was very proud of the painting,

but not as proud as its subject! Harry puffed up his fur as everyone admired the portrait.

Harry watched as the children set off with their paintings to the hall, where the competition was going to be judged. Mr Coe, the janitor, came in to help carry the easels and final pieces of art, so Harry took a quick nap while he could. He'd had a busy day after all.

CHAPTER 10

Who's the artist, Harry Stevenson?

Finally, it was time for the judging! The children filed into the school hall, form by form, and sat down on long, low benches. Miss Gibby hadn't wanted Harry anywhere near Flash the corn snake, so she'd said Billy could bring his carrier into the hall, as long as he made sure Harry stayed inside it.

Harry was more than happy to oblige – he'd had enough adventures to last a lifetime. *From now on, I'm going to stay where I'm supposed to be*, he vowed. So Harry got to sit between Billy and Maya (in his carrier, of course), and listen to happy chatter as the children talked about their paintings. *Everyone* wanted to win.

There was a hush as the mayor, the reporter and the artist came onstage. The children gazed at them curiously, admiring Mrs Singh's magnificent mayoral chain, checking out Mr Dunn's artistic beret and tufty beard, and feeling slightly scared of Mrs Finch the reporter. Harry knew all about newspapers as they lined his cage.

I hope she writes a good article about the school, and I get to read it, he thought.

The judges were accompanied by Mrs Edwards, the head, and a shaky-looking Miss Gibby. Harry noticed that one of Miss Gibby's eyebrows was still covered in yellow paint.

Harry eagerly looked for Billy's painting. There it was, between Maya's portrait of Mack and Scarlett's drawing of spaghetti. The judges started to inspect the artwork – this was it, decision time! They moved from picture to picture, making comments as they went. They said things like, 'marvellous composition', 'great tonality' and 'fabulous lines'. Harry wondered what it all meant. He looked up at Billy and his friends: from their puzzled expressions, they didn't seem to know either.

The judges had nearly finished when Mr Dunn the artist gave a cry of surprise as he stopped beside the last easel. It had been placed at an angle to the others so couldn't be seen from the front. As Mr Dunn turned the easel round to show the other judges, Harry caught a glimpse of smudgy orange paint and his own unmistakable scrabbly paw marks!

'My goodness,' gasped Mr Dunn. 'What an *incredible* representation of a sunset! It's an *astonishingly* powerful work for a child. Such fluidity, such talent! Tell me, what's the name of the pupil who produced this?'

'Er . . . Harry Stevenson,' said Miss Gibby.

'Well,' said Mr Dunn, 'Harry Stevenson has a fine future ahead of him,

I'm sure! What a promising young artist! And so sensitive to choose a sunset as "My Favourite Thing". I am *extremely* impressed. I think we've found our winner, don't you agree, Mrs Singh?'

The mayor nodded. 'I'm no great fan of abstract art,' she smiled, 'but this does have a certain naive charm. It's got a wild, almost animalistic feel, hasn't it?'

Harry purred with pride and looked up at Billy, who was trying not to laugh. Maya appeared to have the giggles too. *I wonder why*? thought Harry. He might have been a 'promising young artist' but he was not the cleverest of guinea pigs!

The competition turned out to be a huge success! The judges were delighted with the art on show and kept congratulating Mrs Edwards on her wonderful, creative school.

'There's so much focus on maths and grammar these days,' said Mrs Singh. 'It's good to see a head who makes space for creativity too.' Your school is simply inspirational, Mrs Edwards. I shall be recommending it for a special award.'

'I totally agree,' beamed Mrs Finch. 'I've never seen zoology and drama taught alongside maths before. It's so refreshing.'

'Erm, that's marvellous!' coughed the head, who was managing to look both sheepish and thrilled at the same time. 'Perhaps you could talk to Miss Gibby about it? She's, um . . . our new Senior Lead for Creativity in the Curriculum!'

'*Am I?*' blushed Miss Gibby. 'That's amazing!'

'**Hurrah!**' called the children. 'Three cheers for Miss Gibby. **Hip, hip, hurray!**'

'All's well that ends well,' beamed the school's new Senior Lead for Creativity in the Curriculum when the ceremony was over and she was enjoying a cup of tea back in the classroom. 'But one thing's for sure,' she continued, gazing at her paint-splattered mug, 'we're **NEVER** having a guinea pig, or a snake, in school again!'

At home in the flat that evening, Harry was giving himself another wash. He still had some yellow paint between his toes, and a splat of red on his bottom that was proving hard to reach. Billy laughed as Harry turned in circles as he tried to nibble it off.

Billy was telling his parents all about the day. It turned out that Harry Stevenson really *did* turn trouble into an art form – his 'painting' had won the competition! Harry's artwork, now titled *Orange Sunset no 1* was going to be shown in a national exhibition, Mrs Finch the reporter had promised a fabulous article about the school and it looked like Jack wouldn't be bothering anyone with his tricks again. Billy couldn't quite decide which bit of the day had worked out best.

'I think I liked the maths most of all,' he said. 'And, speaking of maths, here's another sum for you, Harry: if I give you these two carrots and then three more, what does that make?'

A very happy guinea pig, thought Harry Stevenson as he guzzled them all down.

STORY 2
Stop that thief,
Harry Stevenson!

CHAPTER 1

Sleepover time,
Harry Stevenson!

Harry Stevenson was having the most exciting weekend of his life – and, for a guinea pig with Harry's record, that's saying something. For although Harry only wanted a quiet life, lazing in his cage and scoffing carrots, somehow his hungry tummy always led him into adventures. So far, Harry had ridden a dog, flown across the city while hanging from a bunch of balloons, scored a League-winning goal *and* won a national art competition. But, to Harry, none of those things could quite match up to what was going on now.

You see, Harry Stevenson was having his very first sleepover! Have *you* been on a sleepover yet, and if so, were you excited? Well, multiply that feeling by about a hundred, because that's how excited Harry was!

Harry and his best friend, Billy Smith, were staying at Maya Matthews' flat while Billy's parents went away for the weekend. Maya lived next door to the Smiths, with her mum, Mrs Matthews, and their big shaggy dog, Mack. In return, Maya was going to stay with the Smiths during the summer holidays.

Harry didn't know exactly why Mr and Mrs Smith were away (Billy said they were going to a 'Seaside Soul Wheekender', whatever that was) but, as Billy seemed happy to stay behind, Harry was too. So here he was, gazing out from his cage and enjoying the change of scene.

The sleepover had been a lot of fun so far. It had started yesterday, after school. The children and Harry had played for a bit – Harry's fur had been thoroughly brushed, which he wasn't too keen on, but he'd also been hand-fed spinach, which he loved. Then everyone snuggled up on Mrs Matthews' sofa to eat a takeaway and watch a film. It had been quite a squeeze with Maya, Billy, Mrs Matthews, Mack the dog AND Harry Stevenson on the sofa.

After the film it was time for bed. Maya's room was small, so the children brought sleeping bags into the living room and settled down on the floor next to Mack's bed

and Harry's cage. Billy and Maya whispered late into the night, telling each other spooky stories and making animal-shaped shadows by shining torches at their hands. Harry Stevenson gazed up from his nest in the hay as rabbits, bears, chickens and wolves danced across the room. *It was magic*, he thought. Mack didn't like the wolf shadows though, and growled. It took a few sausage rolls from the children's midnight feast to calm him down!

It was now Saturday morning. Everyone was taking it easy after their late night. Harry Stevenson stretched out his paws and yawned as he watched Billy and Maya eat breakfast, still in their pyjamas. They were making plans for the day: perhaps they'd play with Lego first, then have a picnic in the garden.

Mrs Matthews' phone rang and she left the room for a few minutes. When she returned, she didn't seem quite as relaxed as before.

Something's up, thought Harry.

'Maya, Billy,' she said. 'Mack and I have to work an extra shift today. It's at the Grand Hotel – they need us to cover a big event at lunchtime. I'm afraid you'll have to come with me. I've checked and there's a room they've said you can use and we'll take a picnic too. I'm really sorry to spoil your plans – is that all right?'

Oh no! thought Harry Stevenson and he looked at the children with concern. But, to his surprise, they didn't seem to mind at all.

'Ooh!!' squealed Maya. 'The Grand Hotel!

It looks AMAZING!'

'So you and Mack will be working at the Grand Gala?!' said Billy, almost choking on his cornflakes. 'Oh, WOW! Mum and Dad were talking about that. There's LOADS of famous people going, and the Sparky FC team will all be there!'

Mrs Matthews nodded. 'The League Winners' trophy will be on display too,' she said. 'There's an auction and you can bid to have your photo taken with it. It's all to raise money for the City Hospital. Mack and I are going to keep an eye on things because of all the recent robberies.'

'The trophy will be there too?' said Billy. 'Cool! Me and Harry would LOVE to come!

Can we meet the team, and see the trophy?'

OOOH! thought Harry Stevenson. *This sleepover is just getting better and better!* Harry had seen hotels on TV: they seemed to be all about eating and sleeping, which were Harry's favourite pastimes. He was sure he'd enjoy himself at the Grand. Plus, he'd get to share Billy's happiness as he met the Sparky FC team again.

'Ah,' said Mrs Matthews. 'I'm afraid Harry will have to stay here. Sorry, Billy – the Grand Hotel is no place for a guinea pig. And I'm not sure you'll be able to go near the trophy; the Gala is just for grown-ups so we'll have to see.'

Billy's face fell. He knew what 'we'll have

to see' meant in grown-up speak: NO!

'That's all right, Mrs Matthews,' he said sadly.

But Billy wasn't half as sad as Harry! Harry's ears drooped and his whiskers sagged as he crept into a pile of hay. *I'll be left all alone while Billy has fun,* he sighed. *It's such a shame – and this weekend was going so well . . .*

CHAPTER 2

Listen to your brain, Harry Stevenson!

Harry watched gloomily as everyone got ready for the day. *I wish I was going too*, he thought. Billy and Maya had put on their smartest (well, least muddy) clothes and Billy had even combed his hair – just in case they did get the chance to go to the Gala.

Harry sighed, and settled down to read

the paper. There was a big article about the robberies – valuable and precious things had been stolen all over the city.

Harry eyed his food bowl. True, it was only made of plastic, but that bowl was valuable and precious to Harry. *I'll bite anyone who tries to steal it*, he thought bravely. Then he made an **EXTRA LOUD RUMBLY NOISE** and strutted round his cage, looking as fierce as he could.

'Look at Harry!' said Billy. 'King of the Hay!'

Harry felt very proud. *I can scare off ANY robbers*, he thought. He was about to start another parade round the cage when he heard the rustle of a bag of spinach being opened, and stopped in his tracks.

'WHEEK, WHEEK, WHEEK!' he cried. **'WHEEK, WHEEK, WHEEK!'**

'Sorry, Harry,' laughed Mrs Matthews, 'but I don't think you'd like crisps.'

Harry looked up, disappointed. Mrs Matthews had opened a family pack of crisps, rather than a spinach bag, and was taking out two small packets for Billy and Maya's lunch. Perhaps there was something else in the picnic that Harry could eat? Hmmm . . . sandwiches? Flapjacks? No. Mrs

Matthews went over to the fridge – AHA! This was looking promising! She took out some celery, cucumber and apples. Bingo! Mrs Matthews started to cut them into what she called 'healthy little snacks' for the children.

Oh my whiskers, thought Harry Stevenson. He did like healthy little snacks. It was strange though, he puzzled. Grown-ups insisted on healthy little snacks in picnics, but children never wanted them. What a waste! Mrs Smith *always* put them in Billy's packed lunch for school, and Billy often gave them secretly to Harry when he came home at the end of the day. Maybe that would happen later . . . and perhaps

Maya wouldn't eat hers either? Then Harry Stevenson would have TWO lots to polish off.

Harry watched greedily as Mrs Matthews placed the picnic into a rucksack, which she put by the front door.

'Are you taking any books to read?' she asked the children. 'And what about homework? You could test each other on your spellings!'

The children groaned. They *hadn't* packed their homework because they were hoping they'd be at the Gala instead! Maya couldn't remember where her homework was, but Mrs Matthews wasn't a police officer for nothing and the humans all went off to Maya's room to hunt for it. Even Mack joined in by trying to sniff it out.

Harry Stevenson was left alone. Everything was quiet until . . . oh dear. Harry's stomach and brain began to argue.

Get in the rucksack and snaffle those snacks! rumbled Harry's stomach.

But they'll still be there later, said his brain sensibly.

No, replied his stomach, *they need snaffling right now! Billy and Maya might eat them and there'll be nothing left.*

It's best to stay put, argued Harry's brain. *The cage door is shut, anyway.*

Rubbish! growled his stomach. *It's easy to sneak out – that door is still loose. There's loads of time to scoff the snacks and get back without anyone seeing. Besides, guinea pigs are animals. And animals don't know about right and wrong . . . do they?*

Can you guess which side won the argument?

Some time later, Harry Stevenson woke up in a small dark space. There was no room to move, no light and it looked as if there was no way out either. There *was*, however, a strong smell of cheese-and-pickle sandwiches.

Harry wheeked in panic, thinking of

the spooky stories the children had told. What WAS this horrible black place? Then he heard footsteps and light flooded in. Harry looked up to see Billy and Maya peering down at him and realized what had happened. *Oops!* He was inside Billy's rucksack! From the look of things, he'd wolfed all the children's healthy snacks too. He must have fallen asleep after he'd eaten them. And, from what Harry could see of the room behind Billy and Maya, he'd only woken up once everyone was at the hotel!

Oh, Harry Stevenson!

CHAPTER 3

Room service, Harry Stevenson!

Harry Stevenson sat on Billy's lap, smelling strongly of pickle and brushing sandwich crumbs from his fur. He looked round the room. It was an office, where it seemed the children had been getting on with their homework under the watchful eye of the hotel secretary, who luckily had popped out for a bit and missed Harry's squeaks. Now the children were debating what to do about their furry stowaway.

'Let's keep Harry hidden in the rucksack – then no one will ever find out,' said Maya. 'If anyone sees him, we might get told off. Mum could get into trouble, too: she says that the hotel manager is *really* strict. Look, there he is in that picture.'

Harry peered up and saw a framed photograph of a grumpy-looking man in a smart uniform. He had a moustache that reminded Harry of the slugs he'd seen in the

garden. Under the photograph was a label, which said, MR BEVAN, HOTEL MANAGER.

MR BEVAN
HOTEL MANAGER

Mr Bevan didn't look like someone you'd want to annoy, so hiding in the rucksack sounded like a very good plan.

Harry gave Billy's hand a nibble as his friend placed him in the bag's roomy front pocket, leaving the top open for air and a view.

'Sorry, Harry,' said Billy. 'It won't be for long.'

Harry watched as the children tried to settle back down to their homework. From the way Billy and Maya were wriggling about and sighing, it looked like they were doing maths. Harry liked maths. He wished he could help like he had at school.

'I can't do these sums,' grumbled Maya.

'Me neither!' said Billy. 'Come on, let's go and explore. Harry can come too – no one will spot him in the rucksack.'

'Just behave yourself, Harry,' said Maya sternly.

I'll be as good as gold, thought Harry Stevenson.

Harry peeped out from his hiding place as the children explored. The Grand Hotel certainly lived up to its name – it was very big and

VERY grand! Billy and Maya pretended to be guests, reading the newspaper in the hotel's plush lounge – but when no one was looking they chased each other along thickly carpeted corridors, pressed all the buttons in the lift and raced up and down a vast sweeping staircase.

As the friends set off down yet another corridor, they passed an open doorway.

'Ooh, what's in there?' said Billy.

Inside, Harry could see a dimly lit room lined with beautiful wallpaper and shelves filled with antique books. The wallpaper reminded Harry of a jungle, with exotic leaves, huge flowers, and tropical fruits that made his mouth water. The room glowed in the soft light of lamps set on low tables.

Harry Stevenson sniffed the air. There was a delicious spicy smell in the room so he was pleased when the children went in.

'This is my real home!' joked Billy as he flopped down on a sofa and placed the rucksack next to him. 'Mum and Dad's flat is just my holiday house, you know.'

'It's my home too,' said Maya, sinking into the comfiest-looking chair and sighing happily. 'The whole hotel is. It's called Maya's Manor. But this is my favourite room, where I relax every day. And look, Billy, I've put bowls of nuts and olives on the tables!'

'That's kind of you, Maya,' winked Billy, taking a nut from the nearest bowl. Then he looked around quickly to check the room was empty.

'I'm going to get Harry out,' Billy whispered. 'No one will see him in here.'

It felt good to be out of the rucksack. Harry stretched on the sofa like *he* owned the hotel too and sniffed the air again. The spicy scent seemed stronger here. **SNIFF, SNIFF, SNIFF,** whiffled Harry's furry nose. Billy and Maya were looking at a book about the hotel, so he toddled across the sofa in the direction of the smell.

Aha! There on the side table was a stylish pot plant that had been trained into an elegant shape, and a china dish filled with

dried flowers and leaves. Harry could make out marigold flowers, mint leaves and rose petals. *What a fabulous snack for the hotel guests*, he thought as he sampled the mixture. *This is an excellent place – they really have thought of everything!*

But Harry didn't get to enjoy his snack for long because an angry shout shattered the calm of the beautiful room.

'Get that rat out of my organic potpourri!' yelled a man with a slug-like moustache, storming in from the corridor.

'It's Mr Bevan, the hotel manager!' gasped Billy.

CHAPTER 4

Time for a waltz, Harry Stevenson!

Harry thought that 'potpourri' must be something extra special to make Mr Bevan so cross to see him eating it!

'We can't have rats in here,' spluttered the angry man, red with rage. 'This is a five-star hotel! That little beast could *ruin* us. I'm calling Pest Control!'

Mr Bevan reached for his phone and Harry Stevenson gave a frightened **SQUEAK** as Billy quickly put him back in the rucksack. Harry didn't know what 'Pest Control' meant, but from the look on Billy's face it didn't sound like fun. Harry was glad when the children scuttled out of the room and ran away as fast as they could.

As Mr Bevan's shouts faded, another happier sound filled Harry's ears. Jazz music was coming from the end of the corridor.

'Let's go and see what it is,' he heard Billy say. 'We need something nice after a scare like that. I'm sure the homework room's down here too.'

The children set off in the direction of the music. Harry peered from the rucksack as they followed the sound down the hotel's twisting corridors. Then they turned a corner . . .

. . . and stopped in amazement as they gazed into an enormous ballroom.

WOW!!! thought Harry Stevenson.

Harry and the children stared open-mouthed

at the sight before them. The ballroom had been built for the huge dances that once took place in the hotel, when hundreds of people waltzed the night away in their finest clothes. It sparkled and glittered from every angle – from the gold-framed mirrors lining the walls, to the chandeliers on the high ceiling, and the zigzag patterns on the polished marble floor.

Oooooooooh, breathed Harry. As a guinea pig, he didn't know much about interior design (plenty of hay was all he asked for in his cage), but he'd watched enough TV shows about home makeovers with Mrs Smith to understand that this was something very special.

The ballroom was being set up for the Gala: waiters in smart uniforms weaved between tables covered with crisp white cloths, gleaming silver cutlery, crystal glasses and enormous vases of flowers. Luckily, Harry and the children were peeping through a side door that wasn't used much so they could watch unseen.

'There's Mum and Mack,' whispered Maya – pointing towards the stage at the other end of the ballroom. Harry shrank back into the rucksack, but he needn't have worried because Mrs Matthews and Mack were too busy watching the activity onstage to notice the children. A jazz band was playing, while a group of dancers practised their routine, which seemed to involve a long and energetic conga. Harry nodded his head in time to the music as he watched the conga snake round the stage. But suddenly he blinked and looked again. At the end of the conga line, looking very out of place,

was a man wearing a chicken costume.

'It's the Sparky FC mascot!' laughed Billy.

What's **HE** *doing here*? wondered Harry Stevenson. He'd read all about the mascot in a match-day programme: normally, the chicken strutted his stuff round the edge of

the pitch during Sparky FC matches.

'He must be here to help raise money for the hospital,' said Maya. 'He's not looking very lively today though.'

'It's nearly lunchtime,' winked Billy. 'Maybe he's feeling *peckish*.'

'Billy,' sighed Maya. 'That is an *eggstremely* bad joke.'

'Er, Maya, don't you mean I *cracked an eggcellent yolk*?'

Maya raised her eyebrows as high as they would go. Even Harry thought that Billy had gone a pun too far.

The chicken was doing his best to keep up with the conga, but Harry thought he looked a bit shifty. *He should be shaking his tail feathers with a lot more pizzazz.*

'Come on,' sighed Maya. 'Let's finish that homework. Then maybe Mum will let us watch the Gala.'

The children set off again. But they hadn't got far when they had a nasty surprise.

'Hey!' yelled a familiar and angry voice. 'You kids!!'

It was Mr Bevan and he was holding up what had once been a very elegant pot plant. It didn't look so elegant now – because something (or *someone*) had taken jagged little bites out of all its leaves.

Oops, cringed Harry Stevenson – the plant had made a delicious starter before the potpourri.

'Come back and hand over that fat ginger rat!' shouted Mr Bevan.

'**RUN!**' cried Billy.

CHAPTER 5

Lost,
Harry Stevenson?

Harry Stevenson shut his eyes tightly as he was thrown about the rucksack. He felt like he was in the Smiths' washing machine! He could hear Billy and Maya panting as they raced down corridors, dodging surprised staff and guests – and the heavy footsteps of Mr Bevan behind them.

Luckily, Billy and Maya were speedy runners and started to outpace the hotel manager. The menacing sound of his footsteps grew fainter, then vanished.

Thank goodness for that, thought Harry.

As Billy slowed his pace, the bumping of the rucksack slowed too, so Harry was able to relax and look out again. He saw that they were now in a quieter part of the hotel. There was nobody around at all.

I'm sure we've been down this corridor before, thought Harry as he spotted a familiar-looking vase of flowers on a side table. Five minutes later, they passed the flowers again.

I think we're lost, thought Harry.

The children trudged along more corridors and tried a few staircases, but it was no use. They *were* lost! Everyone in the hotel must have been getting ready for the Gala so there was no one to ask for help. Billy and Maya were very quiet and Harry could understand why: it felt strange walking down long, empty corridors, passing hundreds of closed doors. Harry Stevenson started to worry. What if they ran out of food? He eyed the flowers as they passed them for what seemed like the twentieth time. They didn't look very tasty, but they might have to do. But then what would Billy and Maya eat? Harry gulped. He'd heard that in some parts of the world guinea pigs were eaten for food. *Billy would rather starve than do that!* he thought.

'Ooh, look,' said Maya. 'There's the Sparky FC mascot! He's a long way from the ballroom though: I hope he's not lost too! Let's go and ask, he might be able to help.'

The chicken had a key in his hand and was unlocking a door at the end of the corridor.

'I can't believe we're going to ask a giant chicken for help,' said Billy.

Harry Stevenson watched hopefully as Billy called out to the mascot, but the chicken waddled towards the children and barged past without even looking at them, let alone saying (or clucking) anything!

'Well, THAT'S not very friendly!' said Maya.

There's definitely something not right about that chicken, thought Harry.

'Let's sit down and think,' said Billy. 'I'm starving. Look, we've still got lunch in the rucksack. Come on out, Harry, while I grab the picnic. You can have some of my apple – oh, it's all gone!'

Oops, thought Harry.

Harry Stevenson sat on the carpet and watched with envy as the children ate their lunch. The middle of a long, quiet corridor wasn't such a bad place for a picnic, he thought – although grown-ups wouldn't approve because there were no healthy little snacks involved.

Harry had eaten them all.

'Delicious!' sighed Maya, polishing off the last cheese-and-pickle sandwich. 'I feel better already.'

'Listen, someone's coming!' said Billy.

We're saved! thought Harry, turning to look down the corridor. But then . . . *oh dear.* For what he saw was no rescue party – it was Mr Bevan! Luckily, the hotel manager was concentrating on his phone, but if he did look up he'd spot the children at any moment!

Harry scuttled back to the rucksack and wriggled inside as far as he could. He hid under a crisp packet and shook with fear. Thoughts of Pest Control filled his mind. Would there really be no more Billy, or spinach, or sleepovers? If Mr Bevan found him, it was all over for Harry Stevenson!

CHAPTER 6

Hide,
Harry Stevenson!

'Quick!' said Billy. 'We can't have that nasty man finding Harry! Let's hide in the room that the chicken was unlocking.'

The children raced down the corridor and tumbled into the darkened room. Through the door they could hear Mr Bevan's voice as he spoke on the phone. It got louder and louder – the hotel manager was heading their way!

'We've GOT to hide Harry Stevenson,' said Billy, searching for the light switch. 'Mr Bevan means business – he really does think Harry's a rat!'

Billy flicked on the light and quickly took Harry out of the rucksack. Harry looked round the room. There were no cupboards to crouch in, no curtains to hide behind. In fact, it was totally bare apart from a table . . . and the **big, shiny, golden trophy** that sat on it.

Harry and the children stared in amazement.

It was Sparky FC's League Winners' trophy!

'Hmmmm,' said Billy thoughtfully, and Harry wondered why.

'Billy, you can't!' breathed Maya. Harry was puzzled: what was going on?

'There's nowhere else!' said Billy in a panicky voice. 'I'll just pop Harry in until Mr Bevan clears off. It won't be long, Harry, honest, just a few minutes – and it's a lot better than Pest Control, I promise.'

Harry Stevenson didn't understand what Billy meant – had his friend gone mad? Surely there was nowhere to hide? He gave a confused **SQUEAK**. But, as Billy carried him gently towards the trophy, Harry understood. Any doubts he might have had vanished when the sound of footsteps reached the door. Billy put him carefully in the trophy and replaced the lid. Safely hidden, Harry couldn't see what happened next, but he could hear perfectly well.

'You lot!' said Mr Bevan in surprise. 'What are YOU doing in here? And where's that rat of yours?'

'What rat, Mr Bevan?' asked Billy, and Harry smiled.

Billy can act too! he thought proudly. His friend really was Talented in Every Way.

Harry could hear angry huffing and puffing as Mr Bevan rummaged through Billy's rucksack. But he found nothing but empty crisp packets and a few crumbs of cheese-and-pickle sandwich. Guinea pigs don't laugh, but if they could Harry would have given a little chuckle at that point.

What happened next was no laughing matter though.

'Out of here, you two,' said Mr Bevan. 'The Gala's about to start and I've got work to do. I don't want you hanging around and getting in the way. It's time you found your parents and stopped making a nuisance of yourselves. How did you get in here anyway? This room is always supposed to be locked. Just *wait* until I find the member of staff who left it open!'

Harry heard Billy and Maya saying they could find their own way back, but Mr Bevan wouldn't listen. The children had to go with him to his office; there was no way they could stay in that room. He shooed the children out. Harry heard the noise of a key turning as Mr Bevan locked the door, and the sound of Billy and Maya arguing with him, but the voices grew fainter and soon everything was quiet.

Harry Stevenson was alone in the trophy!

CHAPTER 7

Whatever next, Harry Stevenson?!

Harry Stevenson considered his situation. It was certainly unusual. He was stuck inside a trophy with steep, slippery sides so he couldn't climb out. The trophy was in an empty room so no one would hear him if he wheeked. Even if they did, the room was locked so they couldn't get in. And, as if **THAT** wasn't bad enough, somewhere beyond that door prowled an angry hotel manager, who thought Harry was a rat and had dark plans for him.

Things could be better, he thought. But, on the plus side, they could have been a whole lot worse. The trophy had little holes as part of its design, so there were was plenty of air coming in, and the soft and comfy cloth in its base made it rather cosy. Most importantly of all, Harry had his friend Billy on his side.

Billy is the best, most clever friend, thought Harry. *He'll find a way to rescue me!*

Harry thought about Billy for a while, and other good things, like carrots and beetroot.

Then he snuggled up in the soft cloth and
went to asleep.

Harry Stevenson might have been able to snooze in the trophy, but Billy and Maya were nowhere *near* as relaxed. They had to think of a rescue plan, and fast! As soon as Mr Bevan left to deal with a customer, they raced to the ballroom to find Mrs Matthews. But when they arrived they saw the Gala was starting. The first few guests were gliding in and Mrs Matthews was nowhere to be seen!

The children tiptoed into the ballroom and hid behind a pillar. The room had changed a lot since they'd last seen it: each table was now groaning with food. There were platters of meat, fish, salads, dips, slices of fruit and cheeses. And the puddings looked even better: mountains of cake and fluffy towers of trifle, all dotted with berries. Billy and Maya couldn't help staring – then forced their minds back to the problem in hand.

'We've got to get near the stage for when the trophy arrives,' said Maya.

'But how?' asked Billy. 'If Mr Bevan *or anyone* sees us, they'll throw us out, and we'll never get Harry back!'

'I know!' whispered Maya. 'Follow me!'

With that, she dropped to the floor and wriggled under the nearest table. The starched white tablecloth fell to the floor like a curtain so she was perfectly hidden. Billy grinned and followed her.

'You're a genius, Maya,' he whispered as they sat under the table, trying not to giggle. The tables were huge so there was lots of room underneath. Maya winked and put her finger to her lips. She crawled to the tablecloth edge and lifted it slightly to check that the coast was clear, then scuttled under the next table. Billy followed, and

together they slowly made their way across the room. The tables were close together so it wasn't too hard to stay hidden, and the guests were arriving in dribs and drabs so the children didn't have too many feet to avoid! At one point, Billy made a funny snorting noise as he tried to stop a laugh from bursting out, but the band were playing an especially jazzy tune so nobody heard him.

Finally, Billy and Maya reached the table nearest the stage and peeped out from under the tablecloth. There was a lot to see as the room filled up, and hard-working staff dashed about, helping glamorous guests in beautiful clothes. Billy and Maya gasped as they spotted pop stars and actors from TV shows, but they were the most excited when the Sparky FC team sat down at their table. The children couldn't believe they were so close to their heroes . . . or at least their shoes!

Suddenly there was a burst of music and a famous TV star stepped onstage. Billy recognized him from his dad's favourite antiques show.

'Ladies and gentlemen, WELCOME to our charity gala in aid of the City Hospital. Let the fun begin! We have a WONDERFUL programme of entertainment laid on, folks – you'll never BELIEVE what's coming up.'

'He's right, you know,' said Billy. 'A guinea pig in a trophy? *No one* would believe that.'

CHAPTER 8

Sound the alarm, Harry Stevenson

The band struck up again and the troupe of dancers sashayed on to the stage. They wore sparkly dresses, feather boas and fabulous headdresses. One dancer looked like she had a fruit basket on her head! The dancers swayed in time to the band's tunes, then the dancing and music started to pick up pace.

The band went red in the face as they played faster and faster, while the dancers swirled around them in a whirlwind of glitter and sequins.

'Ladies and gentlemen!' called the host. 'It's time for the charity auction! Now I hope you're feeling lucky because our first item is something very special indeed. It's the chance to have your photograph taken holding . . . Sparky FC's League Winners' trophy!'

There were cheers from the crowd as Mr Bevan and a team of waiters came in with the trophy and placed it on a stand at the front of the stage. They were followed by the Sparky FC mascot who skipped about the stand, flapping his wings and looking rather silly.

Lots of people wanted to be photographed with the trophy, so the bidding was fast and furious. Finally, a pop star won with a sky-high bid, and came onstage to be photographed. The chicken mascot stood beside him as the photo was taken. *SNAP!* Then Mr Bevan and his staff carried the stand and trophy to the back of the stage, while the auction moved on to the next item.

'Keep an eye on that trophy,' whispered Billy. 'We might get a chance to rescue Harry soon.'

'Only if the chicken clears off,' said Maya. The man in the chicken suit was hanging around the back of the stage for some reason. Then he moved over to examine

the trophy on the stand. He looked from side to side with his beady chicken eyes, clucked with approval and then picked up the trophy.

'What *on earth* is that chicken doing?' said Billy.

Harry Stevenson had been sleeping soundly until this point. Now he was woken by the noise of his belly, which was starting to rumble after a couple of hours without food. *Where am I?* he thought – and then he remembered. *At the bottom of a football trophy. Oh.* Harry started to feel a little worried that Billy hadn't rescued him yet.

Time to assess the situation, he thought. Harry placed his eye next to one of the holes in the trophy and peered out.

To his surprise, he saw a pair of very big and extremely orange chicken feet.

Well, that wasn't what he'd expected! He lifted his gaze a little – and saw the yellow-feathered arms and orange-gloved hands of the chicken costume clasped firmly round the trophy. And then he looked all the way up – to see the chicken's head!

What's happening? Harry Stevenson was confused. Trophies and chickens? It was suddenly all too much and he longed for home. *I wish I was back in my cage, with my hay and my food bowl!*

As Harry thought about how much he loved that bowl, he realized exactly what was going on. Nothing precious or valuable was safe, Mrs Matthews had said. Just like Harry's bowl, the trophy was both. That chicken wasn't a real football mascot, he was a robber in disguise – and he was trying to steal the trophy!

Harry's mind raced. He had to stop this bad man. But what could a plump ginger guinea pig possibly do to help? Harry thought hard.

Aha!

There was only one thing for it: sound the emergency klaxon!

'**WHEEEK, WHEEEK, WHEEEK, WHEEEK!!!**' went Harry Stevenson. '**WHEEEK, WHEEEK, WHEEEK!!!!**'

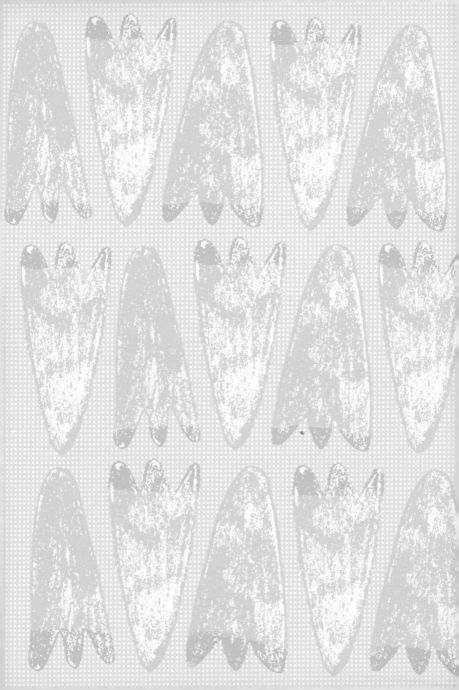

CHAPTER 9

Stop that chicken, Harry Stevenson

Harry's **WHEEKS** were always loud (especially when he wanted food), but the ones he made now were truly ear-splitting. As the noise bounced off the inside of the trophy, each **WHEEK** was amplified over and over again. They sounded like the loudest burglar alarm in history!

This is magnificent! thought Harry. *Hear me roar!* He started to **WHEEK** even louder: '**WHEEEEEKKKKKK!!!!!!!!!!!!!! WHEEEEEEEKKKKKKKKK!!!!!!!!!!!!!!! WHEEEEEEEEEKKKKKKK!!!!!!!!!!!!!!!!'**

The chandeliers above the ballroom began to **shake** and at least two crystal glasses **SHATTERED.** Harry closed his eyes and prepared to make his mightiest **WHEEK!** yet, one that would hopefully smash a few light bulbs and bring them down on the chicken's head. He opened his mouth, took a deep breath and . . .

'**WHEEE . . . KKKKKK! WHHEEEEK! WHEEK!'** Oh no! Poor Harry had lost his voice!

Stunned by the noise, the chicken mascot had stopped dead in his tracks (you could almost say he was a frozen chicken). Everyone stared for what seemed like ages. The audience looked at the chicken and the chicken blinked back. Then the chicken took the lid off the trophy and peered inside.

Who knows what the robber expected to find – but it certainly wasn't a guinea pig! Harry glared up crossly. He saw a flash of surprise in the chicken's eyes but the man recovered quickly.

'Just checking the alarm works!' he joked to the crowd. 'We can't be too careful with you lot!' Then he gave a little bow, shuffled his feet and wiggled his tail feathers, pretending this was all part of the act. There was a confused silence for a few seconds, then some nervous laughter from the audience. Harry heard a few people talk about 'surreal comedy'.

Comedy? fumed Harry in the trophy. *This isn't* FUNNY! (Although it was certainly surreal.)

Everyone had been fooled! Well – almost everyone.

'HARRY!' cried Billy, emerging from under a table with Maya and causing yet more commotion as they did so. Harry's heart leaped with joy when he heard his friend's voice. The two children ran towards the stage, but just as they were about to climb up someone blocked their way. It was Mr Bevan!

'Oh, no, you don't. You stay away from that stage – you've caused enough trouble today! I want you out of my hotel NOW!'

Billy and Maya tried to explain, but it was no use. Mr Bevan would not listen. Pest Control were on their way, he said, and so were Security. The children had to leave the hotel **AT ONCE**.

Helplessly, Billy and Maya watched the chicken mascot pick up a feather boa and shove it inside the trophy to muffle Harry's **WHEEKS**. Then the man did a silly shuffling dance towards the edge of the stage. The robber was going to get away!

'Hey, chicken! Come back with that guinea pig **RIGHT NOW!**' yelled Maya.

WOOF! barked Mack from the back of the ballroom, spotting Maya. He and Mrs Matthews had been patrolling outside the hotel so had missed all of the action. But Mrs Matthews immediately worked out what was going on: she knew fowl play when she saw it!

'That chicken's stealing the trophy!' she cried. 'Stop, thief!'

The chicken turned to flee.

'FOLLOW THAT CHICKEN!' cried the jazz band and singers.

CHAPTER 10

Good work,
Harry Stevenson!

Harry had nearly been smothered by the feather boa, but the robber had actually done Harry a favour. Now he could sit on top of the feathers and peep over the rim of the trophy, holding on tightly with his paws. One end of the boa was wrapped round him so he looked rather stylish. It was a pale pink colour, which set off his ginger fur nicely. Every now and again Harry gave a little SNEEZE as the feathers tickled his nose.

Harry was bumped up and down as the man in the chicken suit ran across the stage, knocking over microphones and jazz players as he fled. He glanced around in a panicky way, looking for the quickest way out of the crowded ballroom.

I can't believe this is happening, thought Harry Stevenson as the chicken jumped from the stage on to the nearest table, then ran across it and on to the next one like they were stepping stones, crashing past table decorations, plates and cutlery.

Everyone jumped out of the way as the chicken laid its trail of destruction, bumping into each other and knocking even more things over. It was **chaos!**

Plates and trays went flying, sending their contents up into the air and back down on to the crowd. **SPLAT!!** Harry was hit by a dollop of flying trifle. He licked it off his fur – yum! Harry stared as the chicken passed Mr Bevan. The hotel manager's suit was

covered in trifle and his hands shook as he brushed a prawn from his moustache. Mr Bevan definitely *wasn't* having a good day.

The chicken reached a doorway and leaped down from the table. **BUMP** went Harry Stevenson. **OW!** A long procession

formed – the chicken with the trophy was in front as he legged it to the door, followed by the children, Mack the dog, Mrs Matthews, the audience, the jazz band *and* the dance troupe, who shed wigs, glittery sandals and feather boas as they ran. The whole procession burst out of the ballroom, charged along the corridor and spilled down the grand

staircase to the hotel entrance. There was a group of photographers by the front door, hoping for snaps of VIPs. They couldn't believe their luck! But the chicken and the chasers swept past in a wave of silk, feathers and trifle. The photographers joined in!

Harry felt dizzy, he'd been bumped about so much. As he scrabbled to stay at the top of the trophy, he saw that the chicken was now running across the high street, followed by the procession from the hotel. The chicken charged past amazed shoppers and Harry saw them rub their eyes, unable to believe what they were seeing (and wondering why the chicken had crossed the road).

Harry heard a wail of despair from Billy. By craning his head round, he could see that some workmen carrying a glass door into a shop had blocked the street, holding up the people giving chase. They could only watch through the glass as the chicken sped off – the robber was getting away!

The robber seemed to cluck with satisfaction – but he'd counted his chickens too soon, because all of a sudden a woman in uniform stepped out in front of him. She was carrying a huge net on a long pole. 'Hand over that rat!' she shouted. It was Pest Control!

The chicken was running so fast that he tripped over the net and went flying! *Oooh!* gasped the crowd as the robber tumbled through the air.

'WHEEEEEKKK!' cried Harry Stevenson, finding his voice as he was thrown from the trophy. He whizzed across the high street, stopping traffic as he flew.

'Harry!' shrieked Billy as his friend soared overhead.

And then . . .

'YESSSSSSSSSS!!!!' yelled the crowd as Harry Stevenson landed in the headdress of the tallest dancer. Harry was safe! The whole crowd danced with joy, and the jazz band played their happiest tune.

But Harry was too busy to notice. The headdress was full of tropical fruit and he hadn't eaten for *ages*.

Later that day, Harry reclined on Billy's lap as the children, Mrs Matthews and Mack sat with Mr Bevan in the Grand Hotel's swishest lounge. The hotel manager was *much* more friendly now he knew Harry wasn't a rat. He'd ordered a Grand Tea for the humans (Mack gobbled up a few of the chicken sandwiches) and a bowl of organic potpourri for Harry! Mr Bevan was thrilled because everyone who'd attended the Gala said it was the funniest, best afternoon ever, and were telling all the newspapers how wonderful the hotel was.

The robber had been taken to the police

station and, when Mrs Matthews' colleagues raided his hideout, all the stolen items were recovered (Sparky FC even got their chicken outfit back). Harry felt very happy for Mrs Matthews because she'd been promoted on the spot, having halted the crime by spotting that the chicken was a 'bad egg'.

Suddenly Harry gave an enormous yawn – and then Billy and Maya did too. It had been a busy day!

'Right, time to go,' said Mrs Matthews.

Harry Stevenson snuggled into Billy's arms as the little group left the Grand Hotel, promising Mr Bevan that they'd come back soon. Harry looked around happily as they walked out of the front door, past the scrum of photographers lining the steps – and into a waiting police car!

What's going on? thought Harry, remembering Mrs Smith's favourite crime shows. *Am I going to prison? I didn't mean to make trouble or eat that plant!*

But Mrs Matthews slid into the driver's seat. 'This is my lovely new car!' she said. 'Let's get you home. Billy, if that greedy pet of yours misbehaves again, I really *will* charge him with causing a public nuisance!'

Harry Stevenson shrank down guiltily.

'Only joking!' she winked. 'Come on – let's go.'

And they whizzed across the city to the flat in a blur of flashing lights and wailing sirens.

Mr and Mrs Smith returned on Sunday evening, and came straight to the Matthews' flat to collect Billy and Harry. They'd had a wonderful time at the Seaside Soul Wheekender. Mr Smith said he'd danced so much he could hardly walk.

'I expect you've had a nice quiet weekend, Billy?' asked Mrs Smith.

Billy and Harry exchanged a look.

'Er, not quite, Mum,' said Billy, handing his parents the newspaper.

Once Mr and Mrs Smith had calmed down, and Billy had explained what had happened for the tenth time, Harry Stevenson lay in his cage and thought about the weekend.

I like sleepovers a lot, he yawned, *but they don't seem to involve much sleep.*

And, with that, our tired little hero snuggled up in the hay and nodded off happily.

THE END

DID YOU KNOW?

Harry's relations around the world are called some lovely names – mostly to do with their small, piggy qualities and far-away origins. For example, in Germany they are called *meerschweinchen*, which means 'little sea pig'; in Italy they are called *porcellino d'India* or 'little Indian pig'; and in Spain they are known as *conejillo de Indias*, or 'little rabbit of the Indies'.

Harry is naturally quite lazy, but he has to do a lot of running around and jumping on his adventures. (It's his own fault. He shouldn't keep trying to snaffle food when no one's looking.) In real life, guinea pigs can be pretty athletic. Young guinea pigs can run when they're only three hours old, while one of the sweetest guinea pig traits is when they bounce up into the air when they're happy. This is called 'popcorning'!

Here are two sporting achievements by guinea pigs from the Guinness Book of World Records:

The longest jump by a guinea pig was achieved by a Scottish guinea pig called Truffles, who cleared a gap of 48 cm in 2012.

The fastest 10 metres by a guinea pig took 8.81 seconds in 2009. This was achieved by a guinea pig with a very suitable name – Flash!

Harry is *very* well looked-after by Billy Smith and his parents. A guinea pig can live up to seven years if he or she is properly cared for. However the oldest recorded guinea pig, called Snowball, lived to the grand old age of fourteen years and ten months!

FOOTNOTE:

Guinea pigs like Harry make the most amazing pets, but they need careful looking after. If you are thinking of owning guinea pigs, make sure you do all the reading you can about how to make sure they are safe, well and happy. Have a look at pet rescues too – there are lots of beautiful, friendly piggies out there needing new homes.

Although Harry Stevenson loves living with Billy, in real life guinea pigs are happiest sharing their nuggets with other little pigs. So once you've found your own 'Harry' to look after, ask him or her to bring a friend!

(And, by the way, once you have guinea pigs, it's probably best to keep your new friends away from classrooms, trophies and robbers dressed as chickens!)

DID YOU SPOT?

Story 1

WHO brings in their pet corn snake for Show and Tell? And who lets him out?

WHAT does Miss Gibby tell the headteacher and her visitors that the class is studying alongside maths? (There are two subjects to remember.)

WHY does Harry climb out of his carrier?

Story 2

WHO are Billy and Maya excited about seeing at the Grand Hotel?

WHAT things do Billy and Maya enjoy doing while they are at the hotel?

WHY does Harry have to hide in the trophy?

CAN YOU HELP HARRY FIND HIS WAY TO THE CARROTS?

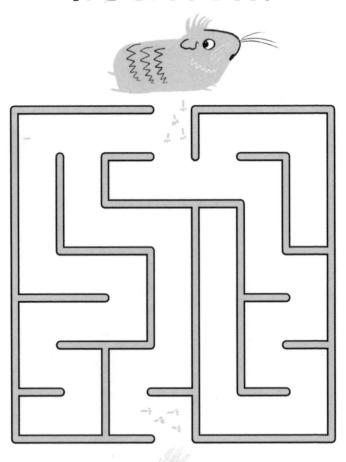

Ali Pye is the author and illustrator of
The Adventures of Harry Stevenson.
These books were inspired by a real-life
guinea pig (who turned out to be a girl
and was re-named Harriet Stevenson).
She lives in Twickenham with her husband,
children and two guinea pigs: Beryl and Badger.

JOIN HARRY STEVENSON ON ANOTHER ADVENTURE!

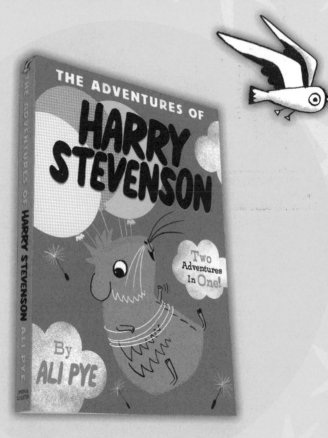

CAERLEON